Royally
REMEMBERED

A ROYALLY SERIES COMPANION NOVELLA

New York Times Bestselling Author

EMMA CHASE

Copyright © 2022 by Emma Chase

Cover design: By Hang Le
Interior Book Design: Champagne Book Design

ISBN: 978-1-957521-91-6

All rights reserved.

This book is a work of fiction. All names, characters, locations, and incidents are products of the author's imagination. Any resemblance to actual persons, living or dead, locales, or events is entirely coincidental.

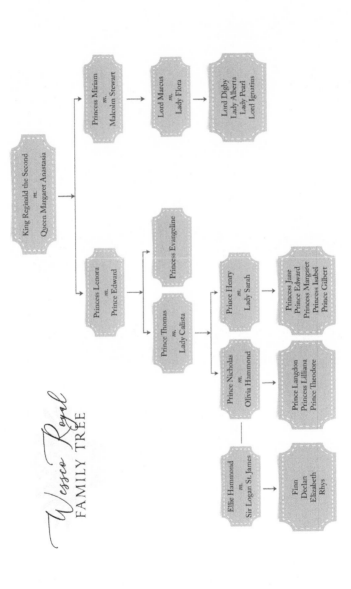

Wessco Royal
FAMILY TREE

King Reginald the Second
m.
Queen Margaret Anastasia

Princess Miriam
m.
Malcolm Stewart

Lord Marcus
m.
Lady Flora

Lord Digby
Lady Alberta
Lady Pearl
Lord Ignatius

Princess Lenora
m.
Prince Edward

Princess Evangeline

Prince Thomas
m.
Lady Calista

Prince Henry
m.
Lady Sarah

Princess Jane
Prince Edward
Princess Margaret
Princess Isabel
Prince Gilbert

Prince Nicholas
m.
Olivia Hammond

Prince Langdon
Princess Lilliana
Prince Theodore

Ellie Hammond
m.
Sir Logan St. James

Finn
Declan
Elizabeth
Rhys

AUTHOR'S NOTE

In the four main books of the Royally series—
Royally Screwed, Royally Matched, Royally Endowed,
and *Royally Yours*—there are moments in the lives
of Queen Lenora, Prince Edward, Nicholas, and
Henry that are alluded to but not shown on the page.
Through the years, I've thought a lot about these moments that played such an integral part in shaping
these characters into who they ultimately became. I've
pictured them in my head—sometimes with a smile,
often with tears. But even in their most heartbreak-
ing moments, there's something profoundly beautiful about the depth of emotions these characters feel
for one another.

If you've read the Royally series books and are curious
about how certain events unfolded . . . the answers to
many of your questions are here.

To the readers who have grown to love these characters as much as I do—this is for you.

Royally
REMEMBERED

A ROYALLY SERIES COMPANION NOVELLA

I

A SELFISH MAN

(Two years after **Royally Yours**)

*"I had a second child, after Thomas—a daughter. Did
Nicholas ever tell you that?"*
~Queen Lenora, Royally Screwed

Edward

"I DON'T WANT TO HAVE ANY MORE
children," my wife says.

Grief is bottomless. An endless chasm
of anguished yearning for all that could have been,
should have been. For more time, more memories.
For just one more moment.

I didn't understand that until now. When we
lost my brother, I believed that would be the most
acute pain I would ever feel. The aching helplessness

of watching him waste away, knowing that when he was gone he would be gone forever.

But I was wrong. There is deeper agony.

"I couldn't bear it if we . . . I won't survive if this happens again."

We buried our daughter today. In a small satin dress and her favorite fluffy blanket.

The service was a spectacle as royal funerals always are, with press and pageantry and miles of black-shrouded mourners. So much pomp and circumstance for such a tiny box. We walked behind her through the streets of the capital—Lenora and I, Miriam, and little Thomas. Before Nanny put Thomas to bed, Lenora kissed his cheek and I patted his head and we told him how proud we were that he had walked the whole way. That he had done his duty as a prince and he had honored his baby sister so beautifully.

And now we lie here, side by side, staring at the dark ceiling above our bed, still wearing our funeral garb because we're too worn out to change.

"All right."

Lenora turns her head to me, and I can feel her surprise before I read it on her face.

"You thought I would disagree?" I ask.

Her voice is curious and soft. It's not Her Majesty the Queen's tone—commanding and stern. This voice is for my ears only.

"Don't you want more children?"

She feels the loss of our daughter in a keenly excruciating way I can't really comprehend. Because she carried her in her body. Felt her grow, knew her kicks and hiccups long before I was ever able to hold her.

And after . . . after we knew she was ill, after the doctors told us there was nothing else they could do—Lenora still hoped. Still thought they were mistaken. Still believed fiercely as only a mother can. Still kept her faith that our daughter would recover.

And I couldn't bear to take that from her. To crush her that way.

I will never not loathe myself for that.

Because when the end came, when the final goodbye was upon us and we held her in our arms as her breathing slowed and slowed, and then stopped—Lenora was unprepared. Blindsided. The devastating shock of it took a piece of her that will never be made whole, wounded her in a way from which she will never fully recover.

"You could've died when you gave birth to Thomas," I tell her. "With Evangeline, it was worse."

It hurts to say her name. And I hate that.

The memory of your child isn't supposed to gut you. There should be delight at the thought of her tiny, perfect face, her little toes, her chubby hands, the way her eyes lit up when she saw us. Her eyes were pale green, but I think they would've lightened all the way to silver. She would have had her mother's eyes if she had more time. If she had lived.

The *ifs* hurt too.

"I won't risk losing you again, Lenora. So, no . . . I don't want more children. You and Thomas are all I want."

She nods, her features pensive. She's still so young—only twenty-four—and in some ways even younger than that. In time, she may change her mind about this and if she does, I will do everything I can to dissuade her.

It's selfish of me. But I have made peace with the fact that when it comes to this woman—her heart, her mind, her body—I am a greedy, selfish man.

"Dr. Abbott said there's a pill I can take. Though the Church says it's a sin."

"I'm willing to take our chances that the Church is wrong. Wouldn't be the first time."

"The pill will prevent me from conceiving, so we won't have to stop . . . we can still . . ." She hesitates, trailing off.

Because in all the times and ways we've touched and tasted and given each other pleasure, there are still certain words that don't come easy to Lenny. It's utterly endearing.

"Fuck fantastically?" I offer.

She closes her eyes, shaking her head, her lips

pulling into an exasperated smile. And then she chuckles ever so gently.

It's the first time she's laughed in months. And it is *everything*.

"You do that on purpose, don't you?" she asks.

"Oh, yes."

"Just to make me blush."

I sweep my thumb across the sweet blush.

"Every chance I can."

Lenora gazes at me, quiet for a moment. Heavy, glistening tears well in her eyes and her voice cracks.

"I love you, Edward. It's very important to me that you know that."

I raise up on my arm and lower my head to kiss her tears away.

"I know. Never doubt that I know."

"We're not going to make it through this, are we?"

And because I understand her through and through, I understand her meaning as well.

"It's not the sort of thing you make it through, sweetheart. There is no finish line, no other side to reach."

"No." She shakes her head and then nods, breathing deep. "It will stay with us. This will change who we are."

"Yes," I agree, cupping her cheek in my palm. "But whoever you are, whoever you become—I will love you every bit as much as I love you now. I will love you *more*."

Lenora reaches up, tenderly tracing my jaw, my lips, with her fingertip. I lie back and she comes to me—nestling her head on my chest, our arms around each other, our bodies entwined.

II

CHRISTMAS AT THE CASTLE

(23 years after **Royally Yours**)

*"His father used to look at his mother the same way—like
she was the Eighth Wonder of the World."*
~Queen Lenora, Royally Screwed

Lenora

I SIT AT MY VANITY, CHECKING MY REFLECTION
in the mirror. Hair, lipstick, straighten the
emerald pendant on the lapel of my snow-white
cashmere coat.

"Are you all right?" Edward asks from across the
room, his arm resting against the thick wood mantel.
"You seem fidgety."

I take a deep breath.

"I believe I'm nervous."

He grins, teasingly. "You? I guess there really is a first time for everything."

I swivel around on the cushioned bench. "Do you think . . . do you think she'll like me, Edward?"

Edward checks the time on his pocket watch. "If history is any indication, I think she'll be terrified of you."

I roll my eyes, turning my back on the impossible man. But he approaches, standing beside me and trailing his knuckle slowly down my cheek and across my neck in a velvet caress.

"You are so beautifully imposing."

Heat blooms in my stomach. Because even after twenty-six years of marriage, that's what he does to me—my dashing, dirty, devastatingly handsome husband still turns my insides to jelly.

"And once she gets to know you, she'll love you, Lenny."

"Yes," I agree, meeting Edward's eyes in the reflection of the mirror. "She's perfect on paper, you know. Impeccable looks, educated, talented, excellent pedigree."

"You had security do a full background check on her, didn't you?"

"Of course I did. She's the first girl Thomas has been truly serious about. What mother wouldn't?"

He presses a kiss to my temple. "One who doesn't

have an army of secret service agents at their beck and call, I imagine."

"Thankfully, I am not one of those."

The shrill ring of the telephone on the table beside the sofa pierces the air. Edward picks it up, listens, then replies, "We'll be down shortly."

Anticipation bubbles in my stomach when he glances back at me.

"They've arrived."

I was born at Ludlow Castle, then visited frequently throughout my childhood—and yet, the beauty of the estate at Christmastime is still wondrously magical. The scent of cinnamon and vanilla waft from the kitchens, and crisp pine permeates the air in each of the common rooms where enormous hand-cut trees, trimmed with glowing lights and sparkling ornaments of red and green, gold and silver, wait to delight all who enter. The doorways are embellished with fresh hanging greenery, red and ivory poinsettias adorn every tabletop, and all the windows are bedecked with lush wreaths and big, floppy satin bows. Snowflakes perpetually drift down from a dove-gray sky, covering the rooftops and treetops in a sugar dusting of shimmering white.

Edward and I step out into the front brick

courtyard just as the shiny black car pulls up. The driver opens the rear door and our son emerges first.

To see him after a time never fails to take my breath away. He is our joy—the holder of our hearts, and the very best of both our souls.

Thomas is tall, handsome, and broad like his father, with my thick dark hair, and has the perfect blend of gray-green eyes that can be studious and serious one moment, shining with laughter the next.

He holds out his hand, assisting his guest from the car. A moment later, she stands beside him—and the photos from the security reports did not do her justice.

She's only a few inches shorter than my son, but delicately boned, slender and lithe, with a natural grace. Her hair is honey blond, her gaze wide-eyed and blue-green. She wears an elegant black overcoat with a knee-length red dress peeking out the bottom, sensible but stylish black low-heeled shoes, and an adorable black wool bucket hat on the crown of her head.

She looks . . . well . . . like a princess. And the two of them together are straight out of a storybook.

They walk to us, smiling—Thomas hugs Edward as my husband pounds his back.

"You're looking well, son."

"You too, Dad."

Next, he leans over and kisses my cheek warmly.

"Mother."

"Welcome home, darling."

Then my son takes a step back, and the girl takes one forward. With a mixture of pride and tender adoration, Thomas says, "May I present Lady Calista Earhart."

She bows her head and sinks into a curtsy, slow and elegant, and altogether perfect.

"Your Majesty. Prince Edward."

"It's lovely to meet you, Calista," Edward says, signaling it is acceptable for her to rise.

She folds her hands in front of her, eyes sparkling with sincerity. "It's an honor to meet you both. I'm so pleased to be here—I know it's not usual. That you typically spend the holiday with immediate family."

It's true. Even my sister, Miriam, knows to bring only official fiancés or husbands home for Christmas—as plentiful as they tend to be for her.

"Yes, well . . . Thomas insisted." I shrug.

I don't mean to sound cold or flippant . . . it just seems to come out that way.

"You must be tired from the drive," Edward says.

"There are refreshments," I tell them. "Come along."

With his hand on the small of her back, Thomas guides Calista up the steps and holds her hand as we walk through the castle.

———❦———

After cider and sandwiches in the great hall, Thomas takes Calista on a tour before settling her into her room for a rest.

In the evening, we gather in the dining room for a late supper, and though it's casual, I can tell my son has educated Calista on the formal etiquette of dining with the Queen. She doesn't begin her meal until I have, and she respectfully sets her silverware down the moment after I do, so the servants can clear one course and serve the next.

Our conversation flows easy and light, as if the girl is already a part of the family.

"Miriam is scheduled to arrive late tomorrow afternoon," I tell my son, in response to

his inquiry.

Thomas grins at Calista. "I can't wait for you to meet Auntie Miriam, Lis. She's an

absolute hoot."

"That's one way to describe Miriam," Edward says.

"Calista, we should go for a drive around the estate tomorrow morning," I say. "Just the two of us, to get better acquainted. I can drive us."

"When did you start driving, Mum?" Thomas asks.

"Just recently. Your father taught me."

"Teaching," Edward amends. "I'm *teaching* you."

"Such a useful skill," I go on. "I should have insisted on learning ages ago. And so invigorating—it feels almost like flying."

"Perhaps a bicycle ride would be better, Lenora?" Edward suggests. "Or a nice long walk?"

"No, that won't do. A drive will give us a better opportunity to chat."

"We did agree that I would be in the car with you when you drive, my dear."

I smile at Calista, lest she get the impression I'm not an excellent driver.

"He worries so."

Edward grins, but there's an edge to it.

"I am a worrier."

"But you shouldn't be concerned," I tell him. "I'm ready to drive on my own now—I'm certain of it."

Edward takes a drink of his wine. "I'm glad you're certain. Although there was that time not too long ago, with the deer . . ."

"That could've happened to anyone."

"Yes, but it happened to you."

I meet Thomas's eyes, explaining, "One moment the road was perfectly clear and the next the poor thing was right in the middle of it. Couldn't be avoided."

"And the incident with the tree . . ." Edward recalls.

"A tree?" Thomas pipes up, looking worried. "There was a tree? Were you hurt?"

I wave my hand.

"It was just a little tap."

"Or some might say," Edward laughs—a bit wildly now, "a major collision."

"Tomato-tomahto." I shrug. "We have several cars on the estate, so there was no harm done."

Edward stares at me pointedly.

"And the lake, Lenora."

I glance away for a moment . . . remembering. Well, there's really no way to put a positive spin on that one.

"Yes, the lake was unfortunate."

Edward pinches the bridge of his nose. Then he asks, "Do you ride, Calista?"

"I do, Your Highness. Though not as often as I'd like."

He raises a brow at me. "You have that beautiful new stallion you haven't taken out yet."

"That's true," I concede. "Calista, would you prefer to go riding tomorrow?"

"I would genuinely love that, Your Majesty."

"Splendid!" Edward claps his hands—a bit too quickly. "So, it's settled—riding it is."

And only then is my husband able to finish his supper.

———❈———

After dessert, Calista bids us good night. Before walking her to her room, Thomas quietly asks to speak with his father and me privately in the library. Edward pours three brandies, and we're sitting in the high-backed chairs that bracket the fireplace when Thomas finally walks through the door. He retrieves his brandy from the tray and sits on the sofa opposite us, one arm draped across the back of the sofa and one ankle resting on the opposite knee.

"So?" he begins. "What do you think?"

Edward raises his glass.

"I think she's completely delightful. An excellent match for you in every way."

Thomas nods softly. Then he turns his attention to me.

"I know you've been checking up on her, Mother. And since I've brought her here for Christmas to meet you, I suspect you already know what I'm going to ask next."

There are few pleasures in life as sublime as seeing your child truly happy.

"But I want to hear you ask anyway. Indulge me."

Thomas smiles. "I want to propose to Calista on Christmas Day. And I want to do it with Grandmother Anna's ring. I know the ring means a lot to you. It will be a sign to the press and the public that she has your highest approval."

"And you're certain, my boy? You only get to do this once, you know."

Thomas nods, his voice solemn and slightly astounded. "I love her. I love her more than I ever thought it was possible to love anyone. I love her so much . . . sometimes I wish she'd leave me."

"Why would you say that?" I ask. "She's lucky to have you."

"Yes, but it's not just me she's getting. It's all the rest that comes with me." He gestures to his father and me, and then around the room. "With us. And sometimes . . . I think about how life would be so much simpler for her—better—if she had fallen for an average man. And I love her so much, I want that for her. A life without all the . . . baggage."

"Your mother came with the same baggage as you." Edward's dark-green gaze alights on me tenderly. "And there's never been a moment that I've regretted marrying her."

Even being born the heir to a throne, I didn't consider myself truly blessed—truly fortunate—until the day Edward came into my life.

And I have every single day since.

"I'll have Mother's ring brought here tomorrow," I tell my son.

His smile is wide and full. "Thank you."

He takes a sip of his brandy.

"Now that that's settled," I say, "on to more logistical matters. Is Calista still a virgin?"

Thomas coughs—choking on his drink.

"Mum!"

"What?" I glance at Edward. "What did I say?"

Before he can answer, Thomas asks, "Do you have any understanding of how inappropriate that question is?"

"Well, given your position, it's a perfectly valid question. There's no need to be squeamish. It's not as if I'm asking to . . . what's the expression, Edward? Get my stones off?"

"Rocks, Lenora," Edward chuckles. "You're not asking to get your *rocks* off."

"Precisely."

But Thomas is still affronted.

"All right then, tell me—were *you* a virgin when you and Dad married?"

I blink at him.

"I don't see what that has to do with anything. I'm a queen—the law doesn't care who sired you, as long as I'm the one who bore you."

"Fun fact." Edward nods.

"But since you asked, yes, I was a virgin." And then, in the spirit of openness and full disclosure, I add, "Technically."

Thomas groans, covering his ears.

"No. Never mind. I don't want to know—you cannot imagine how much I don't want to know."

When it seems safe, Thomas lowers his hands and sighs.

"Yes, Calista is a virgin. *Technically*. Are you satisfied now?"

"Quite." I nod. "It will make things much easier going forward."

"I'm aware."

"And now I'm off to bed." I stand, giving my son a peck on the cheek. "Good night, darling."

"I'll be up shortly," Edward tells me.

As I leave the room, I hear my son laugh with exasperation.

"For God's sake, Dad."

My husband laughs as well. "Count your blessings. It could've been much worse."

On the morning of Christmas Eve, Calista joins me in the stables and we set off for our ride. It's a beautiful day, my favorite kind—no wind and the air so crisp the horses exhale tiny white clouds with every breath.

Calista is an accomplished rider, in form and stamina. After warming up the horses with a gallop across the field, we slow to a walk and speak easily.

"My son tells me you're studying music at University?"

"Yes, Queen Lenora. I adore everything about music—listening to it, learning the history of it, and I dearly love to play."

"What is your favorite instrument?"

She thinks for a moment, her lower lip clasped between pearly teeth.

"I can't choose just one. It's a tie, between the violin and the piano."

"Thomas had violin lessons as a child."

"Yes, he tried playing for me once." She glances at me sideways and her voice lowers, as if she's telling a dirty secret. "He was very, very bad at it."

She giggles. And I laugh with her—because the sound is infectious. There's a genuineness about her, a goodness that radiates from her, that I'm not sure I've ever encountered before.

It makes me like her immensely. But more than that—it makes me want her for my son. Eager for her to wrap him in her goodness, to surround him in her gentle loveliness.

Because there will be dark, cold days in his life— of that I am certain.

And he will need her light to comfort him.

We leisurely ride side by side up a hill.

"How did you two first meet?"

I already know the answer, but I want to hear her telling of it.

"Well . . . I was outside the library one evening, waiting for my ride. The rain had been coming down all day, but it was just tapering off. A lorry drove by and splashed a muddy puddle on me."

"Oh, dear."

"It was horrible," she laughs. "Just like in a movie. I pushed my wet hair out of my face and my books slipped from my hand. And then Thomas was there—picking them up for me, and asking if I was all right."

"Did you know who he was?"

"Yes," she answers shyly. "Though the professors call him Pembrook, as he's asked them to, everyone on campus knows who he is."

I nod and she continues.

"As he'd handed me my last book, I thanked him—and a photographer snapped a photo of us. I asked Thomas if the picture might end up in a paper, with me looking like a drenched rat—and he said probably, but that I needn't worry because I was the most beautiful drenched rat he'd ever seen."

Cheeky boy. He gets that from his father.

"Then he insisted that I let him take me to lunch the next day. To make up for having my photo taken. I said yes, and . . . that was that. We haven't really been apart since."

I bring my horse to a stop at the top of the hill, overlooking a rushing stream below.

"How do you feel about my son, Calista?"

Her eyes meet mine and her voice takes on the same solemnity as Thomas's last evening.

"I love him, Queen Lenora. I love him so very much."

"Why?"

She grins in the way one does when a silly question is asked. When the answer is so abundantly clear.

"He's funny and smart, adventurous and honorable. He's romantic and sweet but also bold, and sometimes a bit wicked. He's *good*. Not perfect, but so very good down to his core. And I love that he can be silly with me—that he can just *be* with me. That I'm able to give him that."

"If things continue to progress between you and my son, it is not an easy life you are signing up for," I tell her. "You must understand that."

"I do."

"There are people who will hate you. Passionately. For who you are, whom you're married to, and at times for no reason at'all. Are you strong enough to bear it?"

Calista looks at the reins in her hands, contemplating my question before lifting her eyes to mine.

"Every life has hardships, Your Majesty. I have no illusions that Thomas and I will be immune to that.

Whatever trials come with who he is . . . he's worth it. The way he makes me feel, the way I make him feel . . . that is worth anything."

"It's just that simple, is it?"

And the only daughter on earth I will ever have tells me, "Yes. When it comes down to it, it's the simplest thing in the whole world."

*

Calista

I'm awakened on Christmas morning by the feel of Thomas's lips pressed against the crook of my neck. He slides his mouth upward, his breath tickling my ear as he whispers into it. "Happy Christmas."

I turn onto my back so I can look up at him. With his green eyes dancing and his smile devilish, he is almost too handsome to be real. I run my hand across the broad expanse of his shoulder and down the muscular swell of his arm.

"Happy Christmas, Thomas."

He kisses me then, his mouth warm and firm, making my body tingle decadently—making me yearn for his weight and the touch of his hands. Thomas has such wonderful hands.

When we arrived, the staff provided me with a

full schedule of our visit. Today it's breakfast in the dining room at nine, then the exchange of presents under the tree in the blue drawing room, clay pigeon shooting on the grounds, then a fireside tea in the great hall, and finally a formal Christmas dinner this evening.

But it's early still and Thomas seems well aware of this, as he tugs at the ribbon that holds my satin nightgown together.

"Of all the presents on all the Christmas mornings I've received, I've never unwrapped one as glorious as this."

He parts my nightgown, the cool air brushing my bare skin. And my breathing turns to pants as he kisses slowly across my collarbone.

And I don't want to break the mood, but can't resist saying, "I've been thinking . . ."

He hums hungrily against my skin.

"Me too. I've been thinking all sorts of filthy things while waiting for you to wake up. You tell me yours and I'll tell you mine."

He licks a wet path along the soft swell of my breast, dissolving my thoughts.

But eventually they reconstitute, as nagging thoughts tend to do.

"I worry, Thomas."

He pauses, lifting his head and stroking my hair.

"Worry about what, love?"

"About your parents. They are . . . traditional."

He snorts. "If my conversation with them the other night is anything to go by, they may not be as traditional as they seem."

"But still, this is their home, and I'm their guest. And they've given us separate rooms. I worry it's . . . disrespectful that you're sleeping in mine and not your own."

Thomas kisses my cheek, moving toward my ear.

"But remember, this *home* has forty rooms. It's not as if they'll ever know I'm sleeping in here."

At that moment, a knock comes at the door.

And then the sound of Thomas's mother's voice.

"Calista? Are you awake?"

Thomas groans into the pillow beside me.

"You've got to be joking."

And panic grips my throat.

"You said she wouldn't come to either of our rooms," I hiss.

"She never does this," he whispers, flustered. "I swear!"

And the knock comes again.

"Calista?"

"Coming, Your Majesty," I call back in a voice that's unnaturally high-pitched. "Just donning my robe."

Donning? Did I really just say that?

I pull my nightgown together and leap from the bed.

"You have to hide!" I mouth to Thomas.

"Where am I supposed to go?" he whispers back. "This bed's an antique—I won't fit under it. They made men smaller in the old days!"

I flap my hand at him.

"Shhh!"

Then I fling the blanket over his head.

"Just stay under there. And don't move!"

The Queen knocks again—making me jump. I shove my arms into my robe and dart to the door.

With time for only a single deep breath, which does nothing to settle my nerves, I open the door. Because this is the first time that I'm seeing her today, I dip into a quick curtsy, then pop back up—smiling so wide my face hurts.

"Apologies, ma'am. I've only just woken up."

Her eyes peruse me. They're astute and all-knowing—and for a moment, my lungs seize. So much terrifying in such a little woman.

"The apologies should be mine, for coming by so early," she says with a tight smile. "But I wanted to tell you personally that a photographer will be here this afternoon, to take candid shots. For posterity."

"How nice." I tilt my head and cock my hip in a feeble attempt to obstruct her view of the bed.

"And . . . I've arranged a stylist to meet with you

after breakfast. She'll bring several outfits; choose what you like best. She'll also take care of your hair and makeup—simple, but elegant, you know."

"Lovely," I squeak. "Thank you."

The Queen's gaze travels over my shoulder, making a beeline through the small window of space that exists between myself and the door.

"But Christmas breakfast is casual. Wear whatever you're comfortable in."

I nod—no longer able to speak.

And just as she's about to depart . . . a sneeze comes from under the bed linens.

And I want to die. I actually might. I may very well self-immolate from the humiliation that's scorching my cheeks.

The Queen raises a brow. Then she calls, "That goes for you as well, Thomas."

I glance back as Thomas pushes the blanket off his head.

And waves.

"Morning, Mum. Happy Christmas."

"Happy Christmas." She looks him over a moment, then gestures to his head. "Do be sure to run a comb through your hair before you come down, my boy. Casual is one thing, but we can't have you walking around looking like you've stuck your finger in a socket. It's undignified."

He gives her a thumbs-up.

"Will do."

Her Majesty's lips twitch, almost as if she's holding in a laugh.

"I'll see you both at breakfast."

"Yes, Queen Lenora," I manage to say. "See you then."

She glides away and I close the door. Then I turn, pressing my back against it and covering my face with both hands.

"I can't believe that just happened!"

I hear the rustle of the blankets as Thomas gets out of bed and moves closer.

"Lis, it's fine."

"She probably thinks I'm a whore!"

Thomas laughs shamelessly. "No, she doesn't."

"She does!" I wail. "And I really wanted her to like me!"

Thomas tugs my hands off my eyes.

"My mother was born without the capacity for subtlety. And she doesn't have a shy bone in her body. If she didn't like you, you'd know for certain because she would've said so to your face just now. Instead, she said she'll see you at the breakfast table."

His confidence and humor soothe my embarrassment.

"You're sure?"

"Completely sure."

I sigh, and wrap my arms around his waist,

pressing against his warm, strong chest—comforted by the thrum of his heartbeat beneath my cheek and the kiss of his lips on the top of my head.

"It won't really matter after this afternoon, anyway."

I lean back, looking up at him.

"What do you mean?"

Thomas's eyes search mine.

"What do you mean, what do I mean?"

"I mean, what's this afternoon?"

He takes a step back, worry beginning to cloud his features.

"Well . . . I invited you home for Christmas, to my parents' castle." He laughs anxiously. "To introduce you to them. I thought it was obvious. When you agreed, I . . . I thought you understood."

He says each word with emphasis, as if they hold a deeper meaning that I'm supposed to comprehend.

But it's a strange thing to have seen the romantic history of your boyfriend play out in living color, on television and in the gossip magazines. Thomas isn't a full-on playboy, but he's dated—a lot. He's had relationships with starlets and singers and all types of stunning women.

To protect myself, I've tried very hard not to expect or anticipate—not to hope or dream. To take him at his literal word, to take each day as it comes and cherish our time together, however long it lasts.

"Yes, it's a big step. I do understand."

Thomas gazes down into my face.

"You really don't have any idea, do you?"

"Don't have any idea about what?"

"Shit."

He begins pacing and rubbing his forehead.

"What's the matter?" I ask.

"Ah . . . nothing, really. I'm just a hell of a lot more nervous than I was ten seconds ago."

"Why would you be nervous?"

He stops pacing in front of me.

And slowly sinks down onto one knee—stealing my breath away as deftly as he's stolen my heart.

"Because I want to ask you to marry me . . . and I'm suddenly very worried that I'll muck it up."

He's adorable. Perfectly, utterly adorable—with his dark, unruly hair, and his beautiful bare chest and rumpled navy pajamas.

"You won't," I tell him softy.

"You're sure?"

"Completely sure."

"I have a ring!" Thomas points at the door. "It's in my room."

"I don't need a ring."

"It's an exquisite ring, Lis."

"Give it to me this afternoon. Right now, just . . . tell me what you want to say."

Thomas Pembrook, the Crown Prince of Wessco

and the love of my life, takes my hand and gazes up at me—his eyes earnest and his smile true.

"I want to share my days and nights with you, Calista—all of them. I feel selfish asking, because there are aspects of my life that will be difficult. But I will do everything I can to make you the happiest woman on earth, because you make me the happiest man. Every day."

My heart pounds and my head goes light.

"When we're done with school, I want us to travel. I want us to see the world together; we have the time to do that. And I want us to have babies— beautiful rowdy children who we'll raise with joy and patience, and who will grow up to do amazing things. And eventually, one day, I want you to . . . watch over the country with me, beside me. I want us to grow old together, loving each other madly the whole time. Will you marry me? Will you be my wife and my queen and my love?"

Tears fall like raindrops on my cheeks as I laugh and nod—because I can't tell him fast enough.

"Yes, yes, Thomas. I love you and I will marry you. Yes, to all of it."

And then he's sweeping me up into his arms and spinning us around and around, bathed in the morning sunlight shining in from the window, as we kiss slow and deep.

It's a perfect moment. A most precious memory.

There will be other cherished memories made in the years ahead. When we tell Thomas's parents a grandchild is on the way, the sounds of our boys' excitement at discovering presents under the tree, singing carols as a family around the piano as I play . . .

But that one was especially lovely, because it was the first.

Our very first Christmas at the castle.

III

IT'S ALL RIGHT TO CRY

*(13 years before **Royally Screwed**)*

"At ten years old, I was still hopeful and optimistic. Still young . . . and tragically innocent."
~*Prince Henry*, Royally Matched

Nicholas

I T BEGAN AS A PERFECTLY ORDINARY DAY. THE days that alter our lives always start that way— without a hint of warning. I had rowing team practice, morning classes, studying, lunch . . .

A quarter of an hour into my midday class, the black phone on the wall rings. Professor Dickenson takes the call, places it back on the hook, and turns to me.

"The headmaster wants to see you, Pembrook."

I gather my books and leave, walking across the quad with two security guards following at a distance. They usually maintain a perimeter around the campus, but sometimes, for reasons no one tells me, security tightens—and today appears to be one of those days.

Headmaster is waiting for me in the open doorway of his office when I arrive. He guides me inside, closes the door, and takes a seat behind his desk while I take the chair in front of it.

"You wanted to see me, Headmaster?"

"Yes." His hand reaches up to adjust his glasses—and it's trembling. "I just received a call from the palace, Your Highness, with troubling news. The plane carrying the Prince and Princess of Wessco has . . . disappeared."

It takes a moment for my brain to absorb the words.

"Disappeared? What does that mean?"

"We don't know. It could be a malfunction in the plane's tracking system. They've been unable to contact them, however, and they were scheduled to land some time ago but have not."

A chill runs through me, my skin growing cold as my palms start to sweat.

"You and Prince Henry are to return to the palace immediately."

Words echo in my head. My father's smooth,

steady voice when he and Mum came up to visit before leaving for their trip to New York.

Look after your brother. He needs you.

"They've tried to keep the news under wraps, but it's beginning to leak out."

I stand.

"Where is my brother?"

"He's at recess in the courtyard. I was just about to—"

I don't bother with explanations or goodbyes. I exit the building, not running, but walking in long, purposeful strides. There's a crowd in the courtyard. A moving mass of dark-blue uniforms—and I know immediately that Henry is in the middle of it.

I push my way through before security can clear a path. In the center of the circle, Henry's blond head is pushing into the chest of a bigger, older, uglier, boy. Their hands grasp each other's jackets, tugging and tearing, fists punching.

The larger boy calls Henry a little shit and a red haze tinges my vision. I grip his arm—yanking him away, just as security gets there and separates them. Henry is panting hard, his cheeks red, his damp hair stuck to his forehead.

"Liar! Tell them he's a liar, Nicholas! He said Mum and Dad are dead."

"He's a liar," I say automatically. "We don't know anything yet."

I put my hand on Henry's shoulder.

"The Queen has called us back to the palace." My eyes meet the gaze of the dark suit closest to my brother. "Take him to the car. I'll be along in a moment."

After Henry is removed from the circle, the crowd goes quiet. Waiting and watching . . . always watching. I adjust my cuffs and turn back to the older boy.

And I slap him with the back of my hand.

A succession of gasps ripple around us, but then there's nothing.

There's no response from the boy before me—he just stands there with my handprint blooming crimson on his cheek.

"What's the matter?" I ask. "You only pummel boys half your size?"

"It wasn't my fault! I was only telling the others what I saw online. He started it."

I smack him again.

"And I'm finishing it."

I grip his collar, leaning into his face—my voice sharp and soft.

"If you ever put your hands on my brother again, I will have the men hold you down and cut them off. Do you understand me?"

He swallows. "Yes."

"Do you believe me?"

"Yes."

"Yes, what?"

"Yes . . . Your Highness."

I glare into his eyes for one beat longer.

"Good."

As I walk away I pull a handkerchief from my pocket, wiping the hand that made contact with his skin.

At the car, a security guard holds the door for me, but before I get in I hear my name.

"Nicholas!"

I turn and Ezzy slams into my chest—wrapping her arms around me and hugging me hard. Simon stands beside her.

"What's happening, Nicholas? The things they're saying . . ."

Things are always being said about us. Silly, hurtful, ridiculous things.

But this . . . this is different.

"I don't know. But I think . . ." I choke on the words, to the only two people on earth I can admit them to. "I think it's really bad."

Ezzy releases me from her embrace.

"Do you want me to come with you?"

"You have exams. Your parents . . ."

"I don't care about bloody exams. And my parents don't give a damn where I am, as long as it's not with them."

"I'll ring you when I know more."

She nods, and then she's hugging me again—
fiercely. And Simon puts a hand on my shoulder,
squeezing. I'm lucky in that respect, to have two true
friends. My brother doesn't have that . . . he only has
me.

They step back and I climb into the car beside
Henry.

And they take us home.

Three days later, the Queen summons me to her office. It's early, the sky still a dull, ashy gray. But there
are guards and servants about, because even though
the palace feels like the loneliest place on earth, you're
never really alone.

As I stand outside the royal office my feet feel
heavy, as if they want me to stay right here, rooted to
this place and time. Because beyond this gilded door
lies something awful.

But then it's too late. The secretary opens the
door and I have no choice but to step inside.

Grandmother stands behind her desk, her back
to me, gazing out the window with her small hands
clasped behind her. My grandfather sits on the sofa,
his head bowed, eyes on the floor.

And it's so unlike him—I can't help but stare.

Willing him to look up at me. Wordlessly begging him to prove me wrong.

"Sit down, please, Nicholas."

The Queen never says "please." Not because she's rude, but because monarchs do not request—they command.

So it's that small, simple word that tells me everything I need to know. And any thread of hope I'd been holding on to crumbles to dust.

Grandmother turns, her gaze not really on me but at some point close to me. Her voice is shaky and soft.

"Your father and mother . . ."

She trails off for several seconds, then tries again.

"Your parents' plane . . ." And again, the words fail her.

The silence stretches on until it becomes its own suffocating, unbearable thing.

"Just say it," I whisper. "I already know. Just say it."

In the end, my grandfather speaks for her.

"The plane has been recovered, Nicholas."

I won't understand until decades later—when I am a husband and a father myself—how excruciating the next words are for him. For both of them.

"There were no survivors."

And for a moment, there's no air, no light, I'm falling down and down—the walls closing in, compressing me. I stare hard at my hands. Focusing on the lines of my knuckles, a small cut at the base of my pointer finger, the translucent white beds of my fingernails. Because I don't want to think about them; I don't want to see their faces in my mind.

Smiling and beautiful, teasing and tender and alive.

I hear my dad's words again . . . the last words I will ever hear him say.

Look after your brother. He needs you.

My throat throbs. I try to clear it, but it only aches more.

"I'll tell Henry."

"You don't have to do that," Grandfather says—making me turn to look at him. The lines on his face have become crevices; his eyes that always sparkle with vitality and wit are dull now. "It's not your responsibility."

Look after your brother. He needs you.

"I want to tell him. It should come from me."

Because Henry can't find out like this—not in this room with these stuttering starts and stops, and words Grandmother can't bear to speak aloud. It's already going to shatter him, but perhaps . . . perhaps if I can say it just right, it won't destroy him completely.

Grandfather stands, his jaw tight and his back straight.

"Then I'll come with you."

The walk to Guthrie House is heavy and silent. Outside my brother's door, Granddad puts his hand on my shoulder.

"Are you certain, Nicholas? I can be the one to tell him."

I grit my teeth and look up at him.

"I'm certain."

He nods, somberly.

"I'll be right out here."

In the sitting room, Henry has pushed the furniture and the rug against one wall, and is kicking a red rubber ball against the three-hundred-year-old plaster on the opposite side. It bounces back to him and when he sees me, he scoops it up, tucking it under his arm.

"Can we go outside yet?"

The palace has been on full lockdown since we returned—a prison of gold and marble. No one leaves or enters the grounds and no member of the royal family is permitted outdoors for an extended period of time.

"No, not yet."

He grumbles, flinging himself back onto the sofa.

"I'm so bored, Nicholas."

My stomach churns with sickness, because more than anything, I don't want to do this. I would give my life to not *have* to do this.

"I need to tell you something, Henry . . . something terrible."

He sits up, holding the ball in his lap, his green eyes wide with innocence.

"What is it?"

I sit down on the opposite end of the sofa, my knees shaking.

"They've found the plane."

"Where was it? Are Mum and Dad coming home now?"

My stomach twists tighter.

"No. They're not coming home."

He blinks, his small brow scrunching.

"Why not?"

My throat burns with tears I will not shed and the words come out in a voice of ash.

"They died, Henry. The plane crashed and Mum and Dad died."

The red rubber ball slips from his hands and bounces across the floor.

"That's . . . that's not true."

I want to close my eyes, but I don't. I look my brother in his tortured face and beg, "Henry, please—"

He stands up, his hands squeezed into fists.

"I'm going to tell Dad."

"Henry, try to under—"

"I'm going to tell Dad you said that and he's going to be so angry with you!"

"Henry, please don't make me say it again! *Please.*"

For several agonizing moments, he's silent. His lower lip quivers, but he doesn't cry. He glares at me like he hates me . . . like he hates the whole world.

"Get out."

I reach for him. But he backs away.

"I want to be alone," and his voice is breaking now. "Just . . . please just leave me alone."

I stare down at the floor, because I'll fall apart if I look at him any longer.

Look after your brother. He needs you.

I leave my little brother standing there and walk back out into the hall, closing the door behind me.

"It's done," I tell Grandfather. "He knows."

"I'll check on him soon. Let's you and I go for a walk now."

"We're not supposed to go outside."

"I'm overruling that edict."

I shake my head. "I don't need a walk."

The weight of his warm, large hand rests on my back.

"I do."

---❧---

Despite my insistence that I didn't need a walk, once we're outside and heading away from the palace, my pace picks up. Like I'm running away from home . . . running from something.

Granddad keeps up, his steps matching mine. Until we come to a stop in a small clearing toward the rear of the estate, enshrouded with brush and shaded by oak trees. From this vantage point, we could be anywhere, a thousand miles away—we can't see the palace, and no one from the palace can see us.

"It's all right to be sad," Granddad says gently. "You know that, don't you?"

I keep my gaze ahead and I don't answer.

"It's all right to cry, Nicholas. I won't think any less of you, I swear."

I look up into his face—it's his eyes that undo me. Not the anguish swirling in their depths, but the overwhelming care and concern . . . and love.

"This shouldn't have happened," I tell him.

"No."

"They're supposed to still be here."

"Yes."

I turn away, bending at the waist, gagging and retching even though my stomach is empty. And I remember a story from the Bible, a story of Jesus sweating blood in the garden of Gethsemane.

43

Let this cup pass from me . . .

"It's not fair," I gasp out, ridiculously.

Childishly.

Because I can't think of any other words to describe this pain.

The incomprehensible loss of them.

My grandfather kneels beside me and pulls me into his arms, holding me tight. I cling to him, crying against his shoulder in great heaving sobs, like I never have in my life.

And never will again.

"It's not fair. It's not fair, it's not fair, it's not *fair.*"

I feel his hand stroking my hair. I hear the raw scrape of his voice and I know he's weeping too.

"No. No, my boy . . . it's not fair at all."

IV

HE MADE ME A QUEEN

(13 years before **Royally Screwed**)

"And that, love, is why we're all so royally fucked up."
~Prince Henry, Royally Matched

Lenora

THE WORLD STOPPED TURNING WHEN THEY told me my son was dead. My heart went cold the moment they uttered the words. It was a blessing, really. To be mostly dead inside, to hardly feel, not really mourn. It allowed me to go through the motions and focus my mind on trivial, meaningless matters. So many details.

It was an accident, they said. An airplane is a machine and even the best machines fail at the most inopportune times. No one's fault. Bad luck. Bitter happenstance.

After we lay Thomas and Calista in the ground, and the sky is starless and as black as our clothes, and Nicholas and Henry are safe in their beds, and Edward and I are ensconced behind the closed door of our bedroom—the world goes back to turning.

My heart begins to beat again.

The memories invade.

And it is unbearable.

I think about Thomas as a baby, his round eyes and chubby fists. I remember him as a boy, the smell of his hair, the sound of his voice, his smile, his laugh—and there's nothing to be done but allow the abyss to suck me down. Everything hurts—my body, my soul—it is all just pain.

Pain so acute, I can only form three words over and over and over again.

"Let me die, let me die, let me die, let me die . . ."

Edward's arms come around me from behind as my knees give way and we sink down to the floor together.

"Lenora—"

I twist around, clawing his shirt, desperate for him to understand.

"I would've died when we lost Evangeline, but Thomas was there. He needed me. Now it's only you. You're the only one keeping me here."

"Lenora . . ."

"If you let me go, I'll fade away. I'll fade away and die and I won't have to feel this anymore. I can't, Edward." The sobs tear out of me. "Please let me go, let me die."

He rocks me slowly, but even his strong arms can't hold me together.

Not this time.

Edward's words are raw with the same agony I feel.

"I can't let you go. I won't. I need you. Nicholas and Henry need you."

"No." I wrench away from him, shaking my head. "They have you. You can teach them to be men."

He wipes at my tears and presses me to his chest, caressing my hair again and again.

"They need to be more than men. Nicholas needs to be a king. And I can't teach him how to do that. Only you . . . it must be you."

I dissolve into my tears.

"He was our boy, Edward. Our good, sweet boy."

"I know, my love. I know . . ."

We don't move from the floor for a very long time. We sit there, wrapped around each other. When my cries eventually quiet, because inevitably they always do, I confess, "We should've had more children. *You* should've had more. Handsome sons and doting daughters. I should've given you that. But I was a coward."

Edward draws in a deep breath and traces my hairline tenderly.

"You have never been a coward a day in your life. I didn't want more. You and Thomas were always enough."

He presses his lips to my temple.

"And now we have Nicholas and Henry . . . and they are enough."

Edward

In the days following Thomas and Calista's funeral, Lenora throws herself into her work. She rises early, even for her, and joins me in bed long after the sun has gone down. I allow the long hours because her work is a comfort—it gives her a renewed reason to carry on living.

Nicholas spends time with his grandmother, adjusting to his new circumstances. And I give particular attention to Henry, because he seems most at risk for feeling forgotten . . . for getting lost in this world. We ride together in the mornings and go fishing at dusk.

Being outdoors and busy is soothing for my youngest grandson—at least, it seems to be.

On the fourth afternoon after the funeral, I visit Lenora in her office. As I approach, I hear the unforgiving, lashing sound of the Queen's voice. And I pity the politician or bureaucrat she's speaking to.

Until I walk into the office.

And see Nicholas sitting in the chair across from her desk. His head is down, curving in on himself, as if she's carving out his insides with every word.

"Our future rests on your shoulders now. I expect you to behave accordingly."

"Yes, Grandmother."

"Any weakness you show will harm us irrevocably. Myself, your grandfather, your brother. Do you understand?"

"I understand."

"That's enough, Lenora," I say softly.

But she carries on as if I haven't spoken—her tone as harsh and cold as her words. Cruel.

"When you return to school, all eyes will be on you, now more than ever. You will not act out or grieve—even in front of your closest confidants. The people will look to you to lead them through their mourning—that is your priority. Your own feelings are irrelevant now."

I've never shouted at my wife once in our lives.

But I do now, slamming my hand on the desk so hard the leg cracks.

"*Enough!*"

She turns to me with the gaze of a cornered animal. Wounded and angry—and dangerous.

"Nicholas, leave us, please," I tell him.

He hesitates, looking to the Queen. And that infuriates me more—that she has drilled this obedience into him so deeply.

With her eyes still trained on me, Lenora nods and Nicholas rises, bows, and walks from the room.

Once the door closes, I move toward her cautiously and speak carefully. As if I don't know her at all. Because at this moment . . . I'm not sure I do.

"What are you doing, Lenora?"

"I'm doing what we discussed. I'm teaching him to be a king." Her tone is devoid of emotion. Frighteningly flat. "This is how it's done."

"You spoke to him as if he is nothing to you. You looked at him like he is no one. He's Nicholas. He's our grandson. He's *Thomas's boy.*"

"He is heir to the throne. The Crown Prince of Wessco."

"But that is not all he is."

She scoffs disdainfully.

"You don't understand."

I step closer and my voice goes hard.

"Explain it, then."

The silver eyes that I adore narrow, sharpening like a blade against stone.

"I had Thomas's whole life to prepare him; there was time to educate him with care. But I am sixty-six years old now, Edward. My father was dead at seventy, Mother at forty-three. Your parents were both gone before your twenty-eighth birthday, your brother dead at *twenty*. How long do you think I have with Nicholas? A year? Five years? A decade if I'm lucky? When I am gone they will come for him."

"Who?"

"Everyone. They will cut off pieces of him, bit by bit, until there is nothing left of his true self. And then they will twist him into what they want him to be, to serve their purposes." She shakes her head, her delicate jaw rigid. "No. No—I will not allow that to happen." She lifts her chin, tilting her face into mine, her voice rising with each sentence. "Not to Nicholas. Not to our grandson. Not to *Thomas's boy*!"

For a moment, Lenora glares at me like I'm an enemy.

Then she glances away, breathing hard, reining in her rage, composing herself.

"From this moment on, I will raise him as my father raised me."

"Because that was pleasant for you?" I bite out. "Going your whole life without a scrap of affection?

51

Not knowing if the man gave a damn about you until he was on his fucking deathbed?"

"He made me a queen! Can't you see that? None of us would be here if he hadn't. I never would've been bold enough to befriend Thomas—I never would've met you. I would have let them marry me off to the first man they chose! But he made me a queen . . . before they ever put that crown on my head. And I will do the same for Nicholas, I swear it. If I have to rip my heart in half to do it, I will make him a king."

She swallows harshly.

"And no one will dare move against him. Because he will be strong, like steel." Her voice thins and tightens, until it cracks. "And nothing . . . nothing on earth will ever hurt him."

The fight and fury drain out of me, leaving me defeated. For the first time in my life.

I lift my empty, useless hands.

"No, Lenora, nothing on earth . . . except you."

And I turn on my heel and walk out the door.

Late that night, after several drinks too many, I retire to our rooms. Lenora is there, in her nightclothes but awake, waiting in the chair beside the fireplace. She watches me in the low lamplight as I open the crystal decanter on the corner table, pour another scotch I shouldn't have, and loosen my necktie as I sit down in the chair opposite her.

And she's not cold or harsh anymore, I can feel it. She's wary and worried, and so very, very sad.

"Do you hate me?"

The bark of my laugh echoes in the glass as I take a sip.

"Never. Silly girl."

"Are you angry with me?"

"No. I'm angry at everything else. Mostly I'm angry with myself. At how I have failed you all."

Her head jerks, finding my eyes in the dimness.

"Failed us? Is that what you think?"

My chest is heavy with remorse and so thick with guilt I can barely breathe past it.

"I was his father. I was supposed to protect him. But now they're both gone. And you, Nicholas, and Henry are racked with the agony of it. If that is not failure, I don't know what is."

She wets her lips and rises slowly, taking the drink from my hand and setting it on the table before standing in front of me.

"You listen to me, Edward Rourke. You have *never* failed us. Not any of us." Her gaze glistens and a silent tear slips from the corner of her eye and down her cheek.

"The only reason I know how to love, the only reason there is joy in my life . . . the only reason I was able to give love and joy to *their* lives . . . is because of *you*. And that could never be a failure. Do you hear me?"

She slides onto my lap and takes me in her arms, holding me close and threading her fingers through my hair. And I let myself sink against her, absorbing the absolution I desperately need.

"It's so hard, Lenora," I whisper into her neck, my face wet with grief.

Because it's still able to shock me. The brutality of living. The heartless cruelty of it.

"It's so very hard."

"I know," she says. "But we have each other."

I breathe in deeply. Inhaling the warm scent of her skin, the strength and sense of purpose she has always given me.

"We do."

"And we'll see it through," she swears. "You and I, together. As we always have."

I look up into her face—my beautiful little wife, my queen, the love of my entire existence.

"Yes, together." I bring her hands to my lips, kissing the delicate knuckles of one and then the other. "Forever and always."

She gives me a small smile. It's broken and sad, just as we are . . . but it's still there.

"Forever and always."

V

BLOODY THANK-YOU CARDS

*(11 years before **Royally Screwed**)*

*"She's a battle-ax with a chunk of concrete where
her heart should be."*
~Prince Nicholas, Royally Screwed

Nicholas

THREE DAYS AFTER THE CELEBRATION OF MY
sixteenth birthday, I'm in the yellow drawing
room being lectured by Her Majesty the
Queen.

"These cards will be kept by your guests as treasured mementos forever. One day, they may be displayed in museums throughout the world."

Because these days, if her mouth is moving in my direction—she's lecturing me.

"And they cannot look like a gaggle of chickens stepped in ink and walked over them. Honestly, Nicholas," she tsks. "You will write them again."

My last two birthdays have been more political events than parties. An opportunity for scheming and strategizing, for bumbling bureaucrats to engage in the time-honored tradition of royal arse-kissing, and for supporters to offer their tithings of loyalty.

I haven't received any firstborn offspring yet . . . but there's always next year.

Because this is my life now.

"Which ones should I rewrite?" I sigh.

"All of them."

"All of them? There's three hundred cards here!"

"Do not whine—it grates on my ears. And if you had done them correctly the first go around, you wouldn't need to write them again. There's a lesson in that, if you'd bother to acknowledge it."

I adjust my voice to a perfectly calm, logical tone that isn't at all a whine.

"It took me two days to write them. I'm scheduled to return to school tomorrow afternoon."

And she couldn't care less.

"Then I suggest you get started straight away."

Frustration punches through me—making me want to tear my hair out and declare any future acknowledgment of my birthday a death penalty offense. I want to get up and walk out. I want to stand up and tell the Queen precisely where she can shove her bloody thank-you cards, and her lectures.

I used to hang on her every word, obey every command without question. Because when you've been flung into the deep end and you don't know how to swim, you'll grasp anything that might keep you afloat. I thought her wisdom would buoy me.

But now I think she just likes bossing me around. Even at this very moment, she can't resist twisting the knife.

"Is there something you want to say to me, Prince Nicholas?"

I literally bite my tongue. It's going to be bleeding by the time I get back to school.

"No, Your Majesty."

I push my chair in closer to the desk . . . and pick up the pen.

"Good," she says, then marches from the room.

I begin writing the first card, but when I glance back at the list, I realize I've misspelled the recipient's name. *Nigel Altringham*—it's a stupid name anyway.

"Fucking hell!" I slam my hand on the desk.

"I could use some air."

Granddad's voice comes from behind me—from the sofa in the rear of the room. He'd been so silently observing my exchange with Grandmother, I'd forgotten he was there.

"How about a walk, Nicholas?"

"I have cards to rewrite."

He stands beside me.

"The cards aren't going anywhere. They'll still be here when you get back. Come on."

The air is cool and windy as we walk through the gardens and past the pond, to the wooded area of the grounds where the leaves have changed to their full autumn colors. Grandfather picks up a thick branch along the way, using it as a walking stick.

"There was a time, when your father was just about your age, that he bristled at his duties as well."

"Dad did?"

"That's right."

We rarely speak of my parents. It's still too fresh, too hurtful, the missing of them too sharp.

"He always seemed to handle things so effortlessly," I say. "He was perfect at everything—the perfect father, perfect son, a perfect prince."

"He told us he was going to run away and join the circus once." Granddad grins. "To be a lion tamer or a fire juggler."

I chuckle.

"No one is perfect, Nicholas. And everyone was young once. But your father trusted that the Queen had his best interests at heart. That there was always a purpose to her demands."

I shake my head, scowling.

"I just don't understand why she has to be an insufferable bitch about it."

And the next thing I know, I'm on my back. Down on the damp ground—my grandfather's walking stick pointed in my face.

"She may be your grandmother, but that's my wife you're speaking about, boy."

The old man actually tripped me. It's a little embarrassing how easily he managed it.

But still . . . I get his meaning. So I meet his eyes and nod.

And he holds out his hand, pulling me to my feet.

"Your future is your grandmother's utmost concern—her only priority. It may not feel that way, but that doesn't make it any less of a fact."

I think about his words—and the indisputable truth I know deep down is behind them.

"And how you speak of the Queen will always reflect more on you than it ever would on her. Remember that, yeah?"

"I will, Granddad. Sorry."

He forgives me with a pat on the shoulder. We turn and start heading back to the palace. As we walk, I feel his eyes on me and glance over to find them sparkling with mischief.

"What?" I ask.

"She hates them too."

"You mean the thank-you cards?"

He nods. "She would outlaw them if she could. She whines every time she has to write them."

"Whines?" I laugh. "Grandmother? You're joking."

"I'm not. She is the queen of whining." His voice goes high-pitched. "*Edward, my hand is sore. Why must there be so many, Edward? I'll never get them finished—never!*"

We're still chuckling as we walk back through the door to the drawing room.

Where the Queen is waiting, with folded arms and a frown.

"Where did you go off to?"

"Just taking in the air," Grandfather says. "It's not good for the boy to be cooped up inside all day."

I keep my head down and slide back onto the chair.

Grandmother's gaze darts between us suspiciously.

"What are you two grinning about?"

I glance up, shrugging.

"Nothing, Your Majesty."

"Nothing at all," Grandfather agrees.

She cocks her head.

"I don't believe you."

My grandfather shifts closer to her, speaking in a low voice.

"You're looking very pretty today, Lenora. Do you believe that?"

Her tone goes a bit airy.

"Well . . . thank you."

"I've always loved this color on you," he tells her. "And the way the neckline falls—absolutely ravishing."

"Edward," she says softly. "What in the world has gotten into you?"

"I'm not sure. Let's go to our rooms and see if we can figure it out together."

Dear God, my grandparents are flirting with each other. This is what hell must be like.

Suddenly the three hundred thank-you cards don't seem so bad.

"You'll be all right on your own, won't you, Nicholas?" Granddad asks.

"Yes, I'm fine. By all means, go. *Please* . . . go."

They scurry from the room, whispering words I'm thankfully unable to hear.

And I sit at the desk . . . and laugh to myself.

"The Queen whines."

Somehow knowing that makes me feel lighter, better. . . and it's all just a bit easier to bear.

VI

GOOD NIGHT, SWEET PRINCE

*(Ten years before **Royally Screwed**)*

Lenora

I SIT IN A CHAIR BESIDE THE TABLE WHERE MY husband lies. His chest is bare, save for the white sheet that ends below the ridge of his collarbone. And the sheet does not move.

I'm just not able to wrap my mind around it. I sit here, waiting. Expecting him to sit up and smile, to pull me into his warm, wonderful arms and tell me it was all wrong.

Some terrible misunderstanding.

He's right here . . . and yet he's not. This unmoving man on a steel slab looks like Edward, but he's cold. So very still.

My Edward is never cold—he's sunlight and summertime.

I should understand these things by now. Life and loss. I have been taught those lessons well. But tragedy always comes as a shock—a devastation that rents the soul.

"I saw him, the boy you saved. He wanted to come to me, to tell me how sorry he was for his foolishness. He knelt before me. And the moment I laid my eyes on him I knew . . . I knew what you were thinking."

I stare at him hard, willing him to get up. *Please, please, please get up*. Because a life without him is unfathomable—to be without his love, his presence, the safety of his arms, the knowledge that even when he is away from me, he is still with me.

"You stood on the bow and saw that dark head and skinny limbs, and you thought of your brother . . . and our son. You saw him going down under the water, and you thought—I can save him. This time . . . I can save him."

Edward always blamed himself for the loss of our children, and for his brother's death. No words or logic could ever truly take that guilt from him. It's the price men pay, I guess—men like him. Men who are protectors and champions. When tragedy knocks, even if there was nothing that could have been done, they carry the weight of it around their necks for the rest of their lives.

"And you did. You dove into that icy water, you crazy man, and pulled him up, pushed him onto the deck . . . and you saved him. You just didn't realize you couldn't save yourself. That your heart . . . couldn't keep up."

The pain of this truth rises around me, wraps around me—tightening and squeezing my throat until I can barely breathe.

And I want it. I want it to take me, strangle me, do me in.

She died of a broken heart, they'd say. And they would be right.

And it would be so much easier. To let go, to be free of this anguish, to fade away into the nothingness.

Why do I have to stay? Why do I have to endure and grieve when everyone else gets to go? Death is easier . . . it's the living that's so very hard.

My eyes burn, blur, distorting my vision as I stare at him.

"I want to be angry with you. I want to shout at you and beat on your chest for being so careless with yourself when you . . ." my voice breaks, ". . . when you are *everything* to me."

I shake my head, breathing deep, a scraping, wheezing sound coming from my strangled throat.

"But I can't. I can't be angry because this is who

you are. It's who you've always been. And I love . . . I love every bit of who you are."

A sob tears out of me. And then I'm strewn across him. Grasping at him, pressing my cheek to his cold chest as scalding grief pours from my eyes. And my heart pleads for him to hold me, the way he always has. Because I need him. I need him now more than ever.

"Oh, Edward. I don't think I can do this. It's so hard—it's too hard. I can't do this without you."

I don't know how long I stay there, weeping and shuddering on him. Maybe an hour, maybe a day. I let go, let it out, let myself give in to the awful despair.

But the one universal truth of life is that after a time, all tears run dry. And there are none left to shed.

From very far away, I hear the soft words in my head, a promise Edward made a lifetime ago. I rise and touch his perfect face, stroking his angles and lines.

And then I say the words aloud, promising them back to him.

"I will never be lost. You will be with me always. The vows were wrong—death can have your body, but your soul will stay with me, I swear it."

I lean down and press my lips to his—to his chin, his jaw and cheeks, and both closed eyelids. And I return to his mouth, for one long, lingering kiss.

Our final kiss.

Until we are reunited. In some other place—a better place—a place where this pain and anguish can't ever touch us again.

He will be waiting there for me.

I straighten up, shoulders back, head high, letting the mask descend—covering me, hiding me, protecting me like armor. I wipe my cheeks and pat my hair.

And I walk to the door.

For a moment, I stand there, staring at the knob. It's hard to open it. To leave Edward here, knowing I will never see his face again. Not as he is now—the face of the man I have lived beside and loved every day of the last fifty years. Nearly my whole life—certainly the most cherished parts of it.

I long to turn back to him, but I know if I do even just once more, I won't have the strength to turn away again.

So I force my hand to reach out, grasp the knob, and pull.

Storm-cloud gray eyes meet me on the other side. Winston—the head of palace security and my guard since I was a girl. He is my only connection to the life before, to the person I was, but will never be again.

Winston bows. And when he lifts his head, his gaze drags into the room toward my husband. For one flash of a moment I see his pain. His face twists with grief and guilt, so much like Edward's, for not preventing the unpreventable.

"He was a good man," Winston says, barely above a whisper.

And it almost breaks me all over again.

"Yes, he was, wasn't he?"

I close my eyes and draw in a breath, deep and steady.

"I have to go upstairs now," I tell him.

"Yes, Your Majesty." He nods, shifting to the side so I may precede him.

And then I move forward, one slow, agonizing step at a time.

To do what must be done.

VII

NOW AND ALWAYS

*(Ten years before **Royally Screwed**)*

"I almost never say what I really think."
~Prince Nicholas, Royally Yours

Nicholas

I LIE ON MY BED, MY HANDS HOOKED BEHIND MY head, gazing up at the ceiling, still wearing the dark clothes I wore all day long.

To bury my grandfather.

It's hard to believe he's really gone. I'll miss him more than I can put into words. Edward Rourke, Prince of Wessco, the Duke of Anthorp, was the best of men—honorable and honest, funny and good. But even more than that, he loved us unabashedly and in a way that was uniquely his own.

I'm sad. I was sad when they informed me at
school what happened, sad when we walked through
the capital, sad when the priest gave the final blessing at his graveside.

But I haven't cried. Not even felt the threat of
tears—not even in the privacy of my own rooms. I
cried when my parents died. In the woods, I sobbed
like a child in my grandfather's arms.

But not today. No tears today.

It's troubling.

I worry that there's something wrong with me . . .
something *becoming* wrong with me. That I'm calci-
fying inside. That one day I'll watch them put some-
one I love in the ground, and not only won't I cry . . .
I won't feel anything at all.

And I think she would be proud of me for that.
And that's more troubling, still.

There's a knock on my bedroom door. There are
only two people in the world who would bother me
at this hour—and one of them wouldn't lower herself to knock.

"Go away, Henry. I'm tired," I call out.

The door opens and my fourteen-year-old brother
strolls in—because, of course he does.

He walks to my bed and stands over me, still
wearing his funeral garb too. He's changed in the more
than three years since our last funeral. His voice is
deeper, and he's grown to be only a bit shorter than

me. But on the inside, Henry is still a boy—wild and immature, selfish and impulsive. I don't know if he'll ever grow up. Part of me doesn't want him to, and is glad that he gets to be young. Another part almost hates him for it.

"She's not in her rooms," he says.

"Who?"

He rolls his green eyes. "Granny."

I check the watch on my wrist, thinking of the pocket watch Granddad had—the one he always carried with him—the one he'll never touch again.

And my sadness pulls harder.

"It's almost midnight."

Henry looks at me like I'm an idiot.

"That's what I'm saying. I don't think she's come in yet."

I rise from the bed, retrieve the waistcoat on the back of my desk chair and slide my arms through it. Henry follows me down the stairs and out the door of Guthrie House, walking up the winding, lantern-lit path to the palace and up to the Queen's apartments.

There's a guard outside her door. His face is blank and dispassionate, but there's a heaviness to his countenance. Because the loss of Prince Edward hangs over the palace like a weighted black shroud.

"Where is the Queen?" I ask.

He bows. "The Queen hasn't come in yet, Your Highness. She is still at the gravesite."

"I told you," Henry says.

I nod, and without another word we head out of the palace. Because my grandfather was fiercely protective of Grandmother. He guarded her like she was something fragile—the most delicate spun glass.

She always seemed more like a brick wall to me, but I know he would want me to look after her. And if I can't cry for him . . . I can at least do that.

We walk through the ornate statue garden, around the pond, past the cherry trees, and down the long path to the rear of the property. Giant, swirling wrought-iron gates herald the entrance to the family plot. My parents are buried here, an aunt who died in infancy, my great-uncle, cousins, and all the Pembrook ancestors in their ancient tombs.

It's morbid knowing I'll be here too one day—right in our own backyard.

The graveyard is silent and still—not even the crickets chirp. Grandfather's flag and flower-draped casket still rests on the platform, the hole below it gaping. Waiting. In the dim light of the lampposts, I spot the Queen, in the front row beneath the awning—exactly where we left her hours ago.

She looks . . . small. Swallowed up by the high-backed chair and her black gown. Winston, head of security, stands straight and tall behind the last row of chairs—just like the Grim Reaper.

"Grandmother," I say gently.

Her gray eyes blink, startling slightly, like she didn't hear us come up.

As if she was somewhere else.

"Nicholas, Henry—what are you doing out here? You should both be in bed—it's late."

"Yes," I say. "Would you . . . like us to escort you inside?"

Her gaze turns back toward the casket, her expression filling with such intense, devastated yearning that for the first time today my eyes burn.

"No. I'm not ready to go in yet."

Henry and I look at each other, and then we nod, stepping forward, taking the seats on either side of her. There's no breeze, but the air is brisk and damp. I remove my jacket and drape it over her shoulders.

She looks down at the fabric, touching the sleeve, smiling softly.

And Henry whispers, "It's all right to be sad, Granny. You know that, don't you?"

"It's all right to cry," I add. Because Grandfather said those words to me once, when I needed to hear them. And I think . . . I think she needs them now. "We won't think any less of you."

She takes a deep breath and shakes her head.

"If I start, I worry I'll never be able to stop."

She takes our hands—both Henry's and mine, holding them in a cold, tight grip on the armrests of her chair.

"You are good boys." Her voice sounds different. It's soft—tender. "Such very good boys . . . and I love you with my whole heart. And if I never tell you that again, know that it's true. Now and always."

She's quiet after that. And so we sit. Together.

The sky darkens further and the silence is finally broken by the pattering of raindrops. It starts off slow, a scattered pat against the awning, against the ground—but then it grows, coming down faster, building into a wet, drumming percussion.

Grandmother looks up, just barely smiling—like the rain is a private joke only she is privy to. "It's raining. Of course it is."

When she stands, Henry and I rise with her and watch as she steps out into the rain, lifting her face to the sky.

The beads of water kiss her face, trailing down her cheeks like teardrops. For a moment the lines on her face are blurred, washed away, making her look younger.

She places her palm on the dark wood of the casket, staring at it, then she leans over and kisses the spot where her hand just was.

I feel like a voyeur—a witness to a private moment not meant for my eyes. But I can't look away. Because this is a side of her I don't ever see, a side I sometimes doubt exists. The unguarded side, the vulnerable side . . . the human side.

She straightens up, staring at the dark wood a moment longer, and then she nods.

"All right, then."

She turns away, wiping her face.

"Winston."

He appears at her side, holding a large black umbrella above her head as she dabs her face with a handkerchief.

"Come along, boys," she says to me and Henry. "It's truly late now—time for bed or breakfast, I don't know which."

Her voice has returned to its crisp, no-nonsense intonation. Her shoulders are straight, her chin is high, and her eyes are sharp.

And there's a reassurance in that. A warm, soothing comfort.

Because the mountains might fall and the seas turn to dust, but Queen Lenora of Wessco will remain . . . outlasting every bloody one of us.

I take the umbrella from Winston, holding it over us, as my grandmother slides her arm through Henry's.

"It's just the three of us now. But we're going to be all right. I'll make sure of it."

We walk out the graveyard's gates and into the palace, together.

VIII

A LITTLE THING LIKE A CROWN

(**Royally Screwed,** Chapter 9)

"She's almost eighty years old and the only person she's ever been able to talk to is my grandfather. He's been gone a decade . . . and he's still the only person she can talk to."
~*Prince Nicholas,* Royally Screwed

Edward

"I WANT TO KNOW WHO THIS GIRL IS, Winston, and her family. You are to conduct a thorough investigation, overturn every stone."

Winston nods, eyes sharp and eager for the task ahead.

"Yes, Your Majesty. I'll begin straight away."

She dismisses him with a nod. He bows and leaves, closing the door to the royal office.

And I watch her for a moment from across the room, arms folded, leaning back against the wall. Soaking up the sight of her the way I always did. The Queen in her element is a fascinating sight to behold.

Then I speak, making my presence known.

"What are you up to, Lenny?"

Her eyes dart to me—without shock or unease.

"I thought that would be obvious, Edward."

I came to her here, in her office, the day after they laid me in the ground. We spoke to each other as we always had—with intimate confidence and teasing tones. Lenora accepted my presence just as I accepted it.

Because some things aren't meant to be understood . . . some things simply are.

"Explain it to me anyway."

I look exactly as I did in my prime—broad shoulders, golden hair without a strand of gray, a shadow of stubble on my jaw that Lenny always found irresistible, charcoal trousers and a perpetually crisp white shirt. And while I recognize that Lenora has aged, she is as beautiful to me as the first day I saw her—a stunning, silver-eyed girl riding recklessly through the woods.

"This *Olivia Hammond* that Nicholas brought

home like a stray, and seems intent on keeping for the summer, needs to be looked into."

No one else can see or hear me; they don't need to. It is in death as it was in life—I am here for her and her alone.

"To what end, love?"

"To the end of protecting him, of course. I won't allow her to play him for a fool."

I chuckle, shaking my head.

"You can lie to Winston and the others—hell, you can even lie to yourself if it makes you feel better—but you can't lie to me. Are you investigating the girl for Nicholas's benefit or your own? So you can have a handy stack of ammunition to break them apart should the need arise?"

"Two birds, one stone," she sniffs, lifting one delicate shoulder.

"Didn't you see how he looked at her, Lenora?" I ask softly.

And my wife's voice goes light for a moment, with the same memories as my own.

"Yes, I saw."

"It was Thomas and Calista all over again."

A smile pulls at my lips, remembering the day our son first brought home the girl who would become his wife. The wonderful mother of his children. How he gazed at her so proudly, protectively . . . adoringly.

Just as Nicholas gazed at the dark-haired beauty this evening.

"No." Lenora shakes her head, snapping out of her reverie. "It's not like Thomas and Calista at all. She's a commoner, Edward. A waitress."

"When did you become such a snob?"

"The day I was born." Lenora stands, looking at me pointedly. "She's *American*, Edward. Unfit according to the law."

I chuckle. "The boy's already gone for her. The law be damned."

She shuffles papers on her desk, denying the truth she already knows. "That would be disastrous."

"Now you're just being stubborn. And silly. She's beautiful, hardworking, salt of the earth. And most importantly, she's as deeply taken with him as he is with her. With *him*, Lenora—with *who* he is, not *what* he is. She doesn't give a shit about his title."

"And therein lies the disaster," she shoots back. "She'll never understand him. She will never comprehend the burdens that rest on his shoulders. She's not capable of supporting him the way he'll need." Lenora moves around her desk, standing before me, her features softening. "Not like you. Like us. You knew just what I needed before I even did. You were my rock and my refuge. And I want that for him, Edward. He'll need it—you know he will."

I raise my hand to touch her—I want so much to

touch her right now. To brush her hair back, caress her face, take her in my arms and kiss her until all her wounds and worries are far, far away.

But I can't.

Because there are rules, you see.

So I lower my hand slowly to my side. And whatever longing or pain Lenora reads in my expression, it gives her the courage to ask me something for the very first time.

"What are you?"

I gaze down into the silver eyes that haunt me.

"I beg your pardon?"

"You heard me. What *are* you? Are you a spirit? An angel? Are you a demon sent to torment me for my sins? A figment of my imagination? I've been afraid to ask, but I need to know, once and for all."

I angle my head and soften my voice.

"What do you think I am?"

"I think I went mad when you died. That my mind fractured. I think you are my psyche's attempt to hold me together and keep me sane, at least in part."

I laugh. A deep chuckling rumbles from my chest that makes her eyes narrow and her pretty lips purse with displeasure.

Because of all the answers she could have given, all the thoughts that stream through her shrewd, calculating, beautiful little mind, I wasn't expecting that one.

After all these decades, she still surprises me.

"Your faculties are in perfect working order, I assure you. Despite our grandsons' most valiant efforts."

"Then what are you?"

I stare into her eyes, my voice fervent with the simple, undeniable truth.

"I am your husband. I promised that I would never leave you, and I always—*always*—keep my promises to you."

We stare at each other for several heartbeats and again, I yearn to kiss her. Possess her. Prove to her that *what I am* is still every bit the man she married—and that she is still mine, body and soul.

But Lenora's eyes shimmer with emotion and her voice goes thin. And once again, she surprises me with words I don't anticipate.

"Have you seen them?" she asks.

"Who?"

"Our children. Thomas and Evangeline, have you seen them?"

I swallow painfully, looking down, and the images and memories her question conjures make my voice go rough.

"No. I can sense them nearby, as if . . . as if they're standing behind a heavy curtain. But I have not seen them."

"Why not?"

I gaze back at my wife. "I will see them when their mother sees them."

She seems comforted by my words, nodding. "Yes. I suppose we'll see them together some day."

"Yes. One day. Together."

I sigh. "Now, back to the discussion of Nicholas and Olivia . . ."

Lenora folds her hands at her waist, a sure sign that she considers the discussion closed.

"She will be a temporary presence in his life and then he will move on. He will choose a woman suitable to his station and his future, and that, as they say, is that."

"Nicholas may have other ideas, sweets."

She waves her delicate hand at me. "Nonsense."

"Even steel will snap if you bend it far enough. Don't push him. If you make him choose between legacy or love, I don't believe you'll be happy with the results."

My wife turns and steps toward the mirror on the wall, checking her lipstick and patting her hair.

"Nicholas would never turn his back on his responsibilities, Edward. On his upbringing, his duty. He is my grandson."

"He's also *my* grandson."

I move up behind her, leaning nearer, close enough that she would feel my breath on the sensitive shell of her ear if the laws of the universe allowed it.

"And once I had you, I would've burned the whole fucking country down to keep you."

I meet Lenora's eyes in the mirror.

"If you think Nicholas is going to let a little thing like a crown take that girl away from him . . . you should prepare to be mistaken."

IX

I DON'T WANT TO SAY
I TOLD YOU SO ...

(Royally Screwed, Chapter 25)

*"I will marry Olivia Hammond . . . or I will
never marry at all."*
~*Prince Nicholas,* Royally Screwed

Lenora

I PUSH THE BUTTON ON THE REMOTE CONTROL, turning the television off before placing it gently back on the desk. There's no point in watching now anyway. Nicholas delivered his stirring speech, turned our entire world upside down . . . and has flown the coop.

Lovely.

I let out a long, weary sigh. Because grandchildren invented exhaustion—I'm sure of it.

I try ringing Nicholas's mobile again, and again he sends me to voicemail.

Voicemail. The cheek!

It's strange, but I'm not entirely surprised. I didn't want to believe it was possible, but a part of me saw this coming right from the start.

Edward saw it too. As I'm sure he'll remind me in *three . . . two . . .*

"I don't want to say I told you so . . ."

My husband reclines casually on the sofa, his hands tucked behind his handsome head.

"Then don't," I snap. "Because that would be rude, Edward."

He shrugs, the devil.

"I'm a rude man. A rude man . . . who told you so."

I rub my temples—because grandchildren invented migraines too.

And it all comes crashing down on me. Parliament, the press, the country, the future. Dear God—the future. What will become of the boys now?

I press a palm to my chest, as my heart starts to race.

"I can't breathe. I don't think I can breathe."

Edward rises from the sofa and approaches me, his tone infuriatingly calm.

"You're speaking, Lenny. By definition you're breathing."

"I think I'm hyperventilating."

"You don't hyperventilate."

"I think I just started."

"I don't understand why you're so distraught," he says almost cheerfully. "You still have Henry."

Henry.

I cover my face with my hands.

"Oh God . . . not *Henry*!"

Edward is a bit taken aback by the outburst.

"What's wrong with Henry?"

"What's *wrong* with him?" I gasp, standing up, the burgeoning panic squashed into oblivion by the opportunity to assert blame. Where it's so richly deserved.

"He's just like *you*—that's what's wrong with him!"

Edward looks at me a beat. Then he straightens the cuffs of his suit jacket and lifts his chin.

"I believe I'm offended."

I shake my head, moving around the massive desk to stand before him. To reflexively be closer to him, even now. Especially now.

"Henry is rash and impulsive."

"He's . . . quick thinking." Edward corrects. "Decisive."

"He's as hotheaded as they come."

"The lad's passionate. Passion is good."

"He's reckless."

"And brave," Edward counters proudly.

"He doesn't listen to anyone. Hopelessly stubborn through and through."

Edward rolls his eyes.

"Well, you can't blame that on me—you're not exactly the picture of flexibility, Lenora."

My voice goes smaller, sadder. The fire of culpability dimming to the fragile flame of worry.

"He's kind, Edward. In this place, kind is not a good thing to be."

"Yes." Edward nods somberly. "He gets that from his mother. Calista was always a dear heart."

And then I confess my deepest fear—my youngest grandson's fatal flaw.

"He feels things. So much. He feels everything. And they will use that against him in ways they wouldn't have dared to try with Nicholas. They'll manipulate him, crush his spirit, take advantage—"

"No, they won't," Edward says sharply. "They won't have the chance, because he has you. You will show him how to distance himself. To separate his feelings. How to contemplate before he acts. You will teach him how to be a king."

"What if I can't?" I whisper.

And maybe, just maybe . . . *that's* my deepest fear.

Edward gazes down at me, smiling gently. Beautifully.

"You can do anything, Lenora. Haven't you figured that out by now?"

I look up at him, losing myself in my husband's emerald-green eyes. Letting his belief comfort me, support me; allowing his endless confidence to build me up and replenish my soul. The way it always has.

There's a rap at the door and I turn toward the sound.

"Come in."

Looking more than a bit frazzled, my secretary Christopher pokes his head into the room.

"The prime minister is here, Your Majesty."

"Yes, of course he is." I nod. "Give me a moment, then bring him in."

When I turn back, Edward is gone. But just for now.

I fold my hands at my waist and a take a deep, cleansing breath.

"All right," I say to myself. "Henry it is."

I move back to my desk and sit down.

"This should be interesting."

X

MY GREATEST JOY

(Five years after **Royally Endowed**)

*"I think that laughter and happiness and all those lovely
little tykes will be our dynasty.
They will be the joys we leave behind."*
~Prince Edward, Royally Yours

Queen Lenora

IN THE YEAR OF WHAT WOULD HAVE BEEN MY ninety-fifth birthday, spring comes early to Wessco. The air is pleasantly warm and the sun is bright. Nicholas and Henry are here at the palace with their wives and children, who are on holiday from school. We're in the south garden, after lunch, enjoying the pleasant air and bright sunshine.

I sit on that familiar white marble bench beneath

the cherry trees, near the cherub fountain—that I still think is a bit evil looking—watching the children play on the grass. Henry trots over, depositing himself in the chair beside me with a contented sigh.

"It's a lovely day, isn't it, Granny?"

"It is, yes." I nod, feeling my old bones creak with even that small movement. "The cherry blossoms were always my favorite . . . but they never stay for long."

The warm wind blows, carrying the children's laughter to us and sending a rush of pink petals dancing on the breeze. And it all feels so familiar. Not déjà vu, but something more. Like a memory—the memory of a dream that sits hazily on the very edge of recollection.

And my aged heart whispers that it's time. Time to have the conversation with my grandsons that can no longer be put off.

"Get your brother, would you?" I tell Henry. "There are things we must discuss."

It's not an unusual request these days. Although I am Queen and Henry will be King, behind closed doors, Henry, Nicholas, and I rule the country like the Holy Trinity—strategizing and planning in consort before settling on a course of action.

With a nod, Henry jogs over to retrieve his dark-haired brother where he stands beside his wife, and they return, taking a seat on either side of me.

Resting his elbows on his knees, Henry asks, "What would you like to discuss, Granny?"

I take a deep breath and get right to the point, because blunt is always better. And at my age, there's no time for beating around the bush.

"I'm dying, my boys."

They're silent for a moment—staring at me with slightly differing shades of shocked green eyes. My strong-willed grandsons are so rarely speechless, it's almost funny.

Then Nicholas chokes out, "You . . . you can't die."

Oh, my darling. He's so very much like me—he always has been. A façade of steely stoicism to cover a beating, bleeding heart.

This is going to be hard on him.

"I'm pleased to know you believe I'm indomitable," I chuckle. Then I reach over and place one hand over each of theirs. "But dying is a part of living . . . and for me, that part is almost here."

I pat their hands.

"I'm not ill or in pain; I want you to know that. And I'm not afraid." I look out over the stone garden path I've walked more times than I can count. "But I am weary. I've lived through more than my share of joys and tragedies, and I have earned my rest."

"If you're not ill," Henry wonders, "then how do you know you're . . ."

"Dying?" I supply when he doesn't seem to be able to say the word.

"Yes. That. How do you know?"

My gaze is pulled back to the path.

"Because I see him all the time now."

The boys glance at each other hesitantly. I can't say I really blame them.

"Him?" Nicholas asks. "Do you mean Grandfather?"

"Yes. He used to just come to me in my office." My tone goes admonishing. "And all these years you boys thought I was speaking to a painting—shame on you."

"Right." Nicholas nods, eyebrows raised. "Because talking with your deceased husband is . . . so much better."

Henry glances at the path, his eyes searching. Then he turns back to me.

"Do you see him now, Granny?"

"I do." And there's a smile in my voice. Because Edward is so very dashing. "He's there, pacing the path and checking his pocket watch. He used to do that if I was late returning to him at the end of the day. He would worry about what was keeping me."

Nicholas swallows.

"Perhaps we should speak with the doctor. Tell him that you—"

"No," I cut him off, my tone clipped. "I have no need of the doctor."

"But—"

"There are, however, things I need to do. Items I want you to have. It's important to me."

Nicholas's and Henry's eyes meet again in unspoken communication—and then they nod.

"All right," Henry says.

From my pocket, I retrieve the oval locket made of gold and about the size of a half dollar. I open it, revealing the tiny hand-painted portrait of a woman with long, dark, wavy hair framing her face and sparkling, jubilant gray eyes.

I show it to Nicholas and he smiles softly.

"Is this you, Grandmother?"

"It is. From my wedding day. Your grandfather had it made."

"You were bonny," my grandson chuckles.

"I was quite, wasn't I?"

I close the locket and press it in Nicholas's hand.

"Keep this as a reminder of who you are and where you come from. Pass that knowledge on to your children—they will need that foundation to navigate this life."

Nicholas nods and meets my eyes.

"I'll cherish it."

Then I turn to Henry and give him a pair of thick, square, black-rimmed glasses.

"These were your great-uncle Thomas's. He was very dear and very wise and the very best person I have ever known. When you are King, there will be times when grave dilemmas are before you and you may not know how to solve them. If you hold these glasses or even put them on, perhaps they will help give you a different perspective and the answer will come to you."

Henry's smile is gentle, and filled with emotion.

"Thank you, Granny."

I nod. Then I look out to the children.

"And Jane, where is Jane?"

Henry calls his firstborn over, and the tiny, dignified nine-year-old comes to stand before me.

"I have something for you, Jane." And out of my pocket, I take a golden chain with a ring on the end. A perfect pearl surrounded by small glittering diamonds on a gold band that until this morning had been on my finger for the past seventy-five years.

"Great-Granny!" Jane exclaims when I hold it up. "Is that your pearl ring?"

"No, dearest . . . it's your ring now."

And I place the chain over her dark head and around her neck.

"Granny," Henry worries, "she's too young. She may lose it."

But I smile down at my little shadow—the girl who will one day be Queen.

"No, Jane is special, aren't you? We don't lose things that are precious to us."

She holds the ring between her fingers and nods.

"I won't lose it. Not ever."

I place my hands on her shoulders.

"Your great-grandfather plucked this pearl from the bottom of the ocean with his very own hands and he gave it to me, and now I am giving it to you. So that you will remember something for me."

"What should I remember?"

"When it comes time for you to marry, you must choose a good, arrogant man."

"Arrogant?"

"Yes. A man who is so confident in himself and who loves you so completely, he'll be perfectly happy to stand in your shadow . . . to watch you shine. Never settle for anything less."

Jane's round eyes look up into mine, with a solemnity beyond her years.

"I'll remember, Great-Granny."

"I know you will." I kiss her cheek softly. "Off you go now."

And she walks back to her siblings, her back straight and head high, like she's already wearing a crown.

I sigh—relieved that my task has been completed but even more fatigued.

"Escort me to my rooms, m'boys. It's time for my afternoon respite."

Yes, these days the Queen naps. *The very indignity.*

With my arms looped in each of theirs, we walk silently back to the palace.

When we reach the door to my rooms I ask them softly, "Do you remember what I told you at your grandfather's graveside?"

"You told us you loved us with your whole heart," Nicholas says, his voice rough.

"And if you never said it again," Henry continues, "that we should know it was true, now and always."

I nod gently, tears of deepest affection rising in my eyes.

"It's still true. Now and always."

I move toward the door.

"Grandmother, wait," Nicholas implores.

They are men now, honorable and admirable and fully grown, with children of their own. But when I turn back to them, they appear as their younger selves. At that tender age when they needed me, so very much.

"Yes?"

Nicholas envelops me in a hug, his broad arms holding me to his chest, warm and tender.

"Thank you," he whispers. "For all you've . . . I love you, Grandmother."

A tear leaks from my eye. Because he didn't need to say the words, but I still cherish hearing them.

When Nicholas pulls back, Henry takes his place, embracing me with a sweet fierceness—the way final affections are always bestowed.

"I love you, Granny."

When Henry steps back, I place a palm on each of their cheeks.

"I know, my boys. I've always known; never doubt that."

My throat tightens, but it is with the weight of my happiness and my pride.

"Watching you both find your loves and make your beautiful families has been my greatest joy. I know you'll be all right without me. . . and that's all I ever truly wanted."

I reach up and press a kiss to each of their cheeks.

And then I lift my head and give them the assuring nod they need right now.

"It's all going to be all right—you'll see. I promise."

With a final tender look, I leave them. Walking through the door and closing it softly behind me.

XI

BEYOND THE PALACE

*(Ten years before **Royally Raised**)*

"When our bodies are dust in the ground and our souls are joined in whatever life comes after this one, the legend of our story and echo of our love will live on forever."
~Prince Edward, Royally Yours

Lenora

THREE DAYS AFTER MY CONVERSATION WITH Nicholas and Henry in the garden, I retire to my rooms for my hour-long daily rest. "A power nap," the young people call it, though that moniker makes it no less embarrassing.

But I've resigned myself to the task, as it does help me complete my afternoon and evening schedule with an alert mind. My maid is supposed to wake me each day, but this day is different . . . because it is not she who stirs me.

I'm pulled from sleep by the touch of warm, familiar skin. The sensations of a fingertip running softly along my brow, dragging down the bridge of my nose, and reverently tracing the shape of my lips.

And a voice. A deep, beautiful, teasing voice.

"It's time to wake up now, Lenny."

Slowly, my eyes blink open. Everything seems hazy and disorienting at first—the way it is when one is roused from the depths of a dream.

A moment later, I blink my eyes again, to clear my vision, so I can be sure that what I'm seeing is not an illusion or a figment of my imagination.

Because he's here, gazing down at me with the same emerald eyes and magnetic smile that he wore the very first time he looked at me.

Edward.

My Edward.

His hair is thick and golden and falls over his forehead in that delightfully rakish way.

"Edward?"

His smile grows broader and injects my soul with a joyous, keening desire that I'd almost forgot was possible.

"Hello, love."

Edward takes a step back from the bed and I lift my head from the pillow. I immediately notice that I feel different. There is no ache in my joints, no creaking of my bones like an old door on a rusty hinge—not anymore. And there's no pain. The bodily soreness that is the constant companion of advanced age is gone.

I feel nimble and lissome and energetic—like I could climb a mountain.

Like I could fly if I wanted to.

I look down at myself and realize I'm not wearing the nightdress and robe I went to sleep in. They've been replaced by a pale yellow party dress, with ribbons tied at my shoulders, a lovely silk bodice that cinches at the waist and hugs my breasts, and a shimmering skirt poufed up with layers of crinoline that falls to my knees.

It's an exquisite dress . . . a young woman's dress.

My gaze drifts over my bare arms. The firm glowing skin, without a hint of age spots or wrinkles. Carefully, I run a hand over my hair—it's wavy and long, pulled back on the sides with a clasp in the back in Edward's favorite style. I grasp the ends with my fingers—mesmerized by the shiny, dark strands—not a hint of gray to be found.

"My goodness, look at me."

Edward's voice is devilishly suggestive.

"Oh, I'm looking, believe me. I can't take my eyes off you."

I turn my hands this way and that—amazed at their smoothness and dexterity.

"Am I dreaming, Edward?"

"No," he answers softly. "You're not dreaming, sweetheart."

I lift my gaze to his.

"This is real? You're here and I'm here? And it's all real? Truly?"

His smile is so tender, so all-encompassingly loving, it takes my breath away.

"Come here, Lenora, and I'll show you just how real it is."

I rise from the bed on steady legs. We gaze at each other for a moment, and then I'm moving to him—flinging myself at him. He catches me in his strong, perfect arms, laughing, and spinning us in a circle.

Tears of sweetest joy and relief spring into my eyes.

"You're here! You're really here!"

"I'm here, Lenora," he croons. "Right here with you, my lovely girl."

He sets me on my feet, dipping his head to kiss my forehead and then each closed eyelid, my nose, my cheeks—his breath a feather-light brush along my skin. Then Edward presses his lips to mine, deeply and passionately, his hands grasping my lower back, pulling me to him and molding our bodies together.

His tongue is wet and warm, the press of his mouth hungry and decadent.

I sigh against his lips. "I want to kiss you forever."

A chuckle vibrates in his throat. "I can arrange that—and it definitely won't just be kissing."

I tilt my head back, laughing. "How I've missed you. I know you were with me, but it wasn't the same—it wasn't this. I've missed you so much."

"And I've missed you." He kisses me again, with an urgency that makes my heart gallop and my head swim. "But we're together now—and we'll never be parted again."

"Yes, yes," I whisper. "Never again."

I run my palms along the swells of his arms, his broad, solid shoulders, combing my fingers through his thick hair. My love, my life.

And then we're kissing again—with the fervency of true love in its first, full bloom.

A needy groan rumbles from Edward's chest. And oh . . . I've missed that sound too.

Several moments later, our kisses slow, and we stand breathing against one another, holding each other—Edward's lips resting against my brow.

"What happens now?" I ask him.

"Now, we move on. To our next adventure. Beyond the palace."

"Beyond the palace," I breathe out. "What wondrous words."

"They're all waiting for us," Edward tells me, caressing my hair. "Your mother and father and your sister Miriam, my brother Thomas and Michael, and dear old Alfie. Evangeline is waiting for you there, and Calista and Thomas."

I close my eyes, feeling the bliss of it. I have waited so long for them. Yearned for my children so deeply, there aren't words to describe it.

Edward kisses my hand and moves toward the door. But I tug him back, turning to the window.

"Wait. I want to look at them one last time."

We walk to the window and push the curtain aside, gazing down into the garden where our grandchildren and great-grandchildren are enjoying the sweet air of the sunlit afternoon. Nicholas stands with his arm draped leisurely across his wife, Olivia's, shoulders. They watch their daughter, Lilliana, performing a dance she just made up, while her twin brother, Langdon, sits reading against a tree trunk and his little brother, Theo, climbs in the branches above him. Olivia's sister, Ellie, stands beside her husband, Logan, as he holds their smallest boy, and their other children, Finn, Declan, and Elizabeth, run about. Henry kicks a ball to his son, Edward, while his young daughters, Maggie and Isabel, chase each other in a game of tag nearby.

We watch them all for a time, until I say, "They're going to be just fine without us now, aren't they?"

"Oh yes," Edward promises. "They're going to be outstanding."

Just then, feisty little Jane, Henry's firstborn and heir to the throne now—though they don't yet know it—stops in her tracks. And peers up at the window.

Up at us.

She has her mother's big brown eyes, with flecks of her father's green.

Her head tilts slightly, as if she's figuring out a puzzle . . . and then she smiles and waves.

Edward lifts his hand, waving back, and I place a kiss on my fingers, blowing it to her. With a laugh, Jane reaches her hand out to catch it, before pressing her palm over her heart.

Her mother, Sarah, walks up to her. I watch her lips move and though I can't hear her, I know just what she's saying.

"Who are you waving to, Jane?"

"Great-Granny and Granddad."

Sarah adjusts her wire-rimmed glasses and searches the palace windows.

"Don't you see them, Mummy?" Jane asks.

But Sarah doesn't see. Shaking her head, she grins down at her daughter and holds out her hand.

"Come along now, darling. It's time to go inside."

Jane takes her mother's hand and wraps the other around the pearl ring that hangs from her neck, as they skip away.

I turn to Edward, running my knuckle along the scruff of his fine jaw, then stroking my hands down his chest—feeling the steady, strong beat of his heart beneath my palm.

He's warm and solid, gloriously alive . . . and all mine. Just as I am his.

Forever and always.

"I'm ready now."

Side by side and hand in hand, we walk to the door. Edward opens it, and we step out of the room and into the bright, golden light on the other side.

Into our eternity, together.

The End

ALSO BY
EMMA CHASE

Dirty Charmer

GETTING SOME SERIES
Getting Schooled
Getting Played
Getting Real

THE ROYALLY SERIES
Royally Screwed
Royally Matched
Royally Endowed
Royally Raised
Royally Yours

Royally Series Collection

THE LEGAL BRIEFS SERIES
Overruled
Sustained
Appealed
Sidebarred

THE TANGLED SERIES

Tangled

Twisted

Tamed

Tied

Holy Frigging Matrimony

It's a Wonderful Tangled Christmas Carol

ABOUT THE AUTHOR

New York Times and *USA Today* bestselling author, Emma Chase, writes contemporary romance filled with heat, heart and laugh-out-loud humor. Her stories are known for their clever banter, sexy, swoon-worthy moments, and hilariously authentic male POV's.

Emma lives in New Jersey with her amazing husband, two awesome children, and two adorable but badly behaved dogs. She has a long-standing love/hate relationship with caffeine.

Follow her online:

Twitter: twitter.com/emmachse
Facebook: facebook.com/AuthorEmmaChase
Instagram: instagram.com/authoremmachase
Website: authoremmachase.com

Subscribe to my mailing list for the latest book news, exclusive teasers, freebies & giveaways!
authoremmachase.com/newsletter

Made in the USA
Monee, IL
10 April 2022

94449269R00069